Poppy's Project

by Jackie Walter and John & Gus Art

W
FRANKLIN WATTS
LONDON • SYDNEY

Poppy came out of school.
She ran to Dad and Max.

"We are going to do a project
about families," said Poppy.
"Will you help me?"

Poppy told Mum about the project.
"You and Dad can help me,"
she said.

"Let's make our house
out of boxes," said Poppy.
"Yes," said Dad.
"You need to collect some boxes.
Put them in here."

Poppy put some boxes

into the cupboard every day.

On Saturday, Poppy was ready
to make her house.
She went to the cupboard.
But the boxes had gone!

"I'm sorry," said Mum.
"I put them in the bin.
Did you want the boxes
for your project?"

"You can paint a family tree,"
said Mum.

"Yes," said Poppy. "I will do that."

Poppy painted a big tree.
"I will put the names on
when it is dry," she said.

On Sunday, Poppy went
to get her painting.

"Oh no!" said Poppy.
"Look at my tree!"

Poppy ran to her bedroom.

"I can't do my project now,"

she said.

She cried and cried.

Mum and Dad had an idea.

They got a box

and took it into Poppy's bedroom.

Max went too.

Poppy and Max
looked at the photos.

"This is you," said Mum.
"Here you are on the beach."

"And this is you, Max!" said Dad.

Poppy looked at the photos.

"I will make a photo book,"
she said.
"My project will be
the best project ever!"

Story trail

Start

Start at the beginning of the story trail. Ask your child to retell the story in their own words, pointing to each picture in turn to recall the sequence of events.

Independent Reading

This series is designed to provide an opportunity for your child to read on their own. These notes are written for you to help your child choose a book and to read it independently.

In school, your child's teacher will often be using reading books which have been banded to support the process of learning to read. Use the book band colour your child is reading in school to help you make a good choice. *Poppy's Project* is a good choice for children reading at Green Band in their classroom to read independently.

The aim of independent reading is to read this book with ease, so that your child enjoys the story and relates it to their own experiences.

About the book

Poppy has a school project to complete at home. She has some great ideas, but things keep going wrong. Poppy gets very upset, but luckily Mum and Dad have a good idea too.

Before reading

Help your child to learn how to make good choices by asking:
"Why did you choose this book? Why do you think you will enjoy it?"
Look at the cover together and ask: "What do you think the story will be about?" Support your child to think of what they already know about the story context. Read the title aloud and ask: "What do you think Poppy is doing on the cover of the book?"
Remind your child that they can try to sound out the letters to make a word if they get stuck.
Decide together whether your child will read the story independently or read it aloud to you.

During reading

If reading aloud, support your child if they hesitate or ask for help by telling the word. Remind your child of what they know and what they can do independently.

If reading to themselves, remind your child that they can come and ask for your help if stuck.

After reading

Support comprehension by asking your child to tell you about the story. Use the story trail to encourage your child to retell the story in the right sequence, in their own words.

Help your child think about the messages in the book that go beyond the story and ask: "Why does Poppy think that making a photo book is going to be really great?"

Give your child a chance to respond to the story: "Did you have a favourite part? Have you had to do a project for school? Did you enjoy doing it?"

Extending learning

Help your child understand the story structure by using the same sentence patterning and adding different elements. "Let's make up a new story about Poppy doing another project for school. What will her project be about this time? What might she choose to do or make? How might this go wrong? And how can she fix it?" In the classroom, your child's teacher may be teaching polysyllabic words (words with more than one syllable).

There are many in this book that you could look at with your child: Popp/y, pro/ject, fam/i/lies, box/es, Sat/ur/day, Sun/day, bed/room.

Franklin Watts
First published in Great Britain in 2017
by The Watts Publishing Group

Copyright © The Watts Publishing Group 2017

Series Editors: Jackie Hamley and Melanie Palmer
Series Advisors: Dr Sue Bodman and Glen Franklin
Series Designer: Peter Scoulding

A CIP catalogue record for this book is
available from the British Library.

ISBN 978 1 4451 5445 9 (hbk)
ISBN 978 1 4451 5446 6 (pbk)
ISBN 978 1 4451 6096 2 (library ebook)

Printed in China

Franklin Watts
An imprint of
Hachette Children's Group
Part of The Watts Publishing Group
Carmelite House
50 Victoria Embankment
London EC4Y 0DZ

An Hachette UK Company
www.hachette.co.uk

www.franklinwatts.co.uk